# Decoding the

# MAYAN MARVELS

by Katrina O'Neill
illustrated by Brenda Cantell

TM
**sundance**
A Haights Cross Communications Company

Published by Sundance Publishing
One Beeman Road
P.O. Box 740
Northborough, MA 01532-0740
800-343-8204
www.sundancepub.com

Copyright © text Katrina O'Neill
Copyright © illustrations Brenda Cantell

First published as Treasure Trackers by
Blake Education, Locked Bag 2022, Glebe 2037, Australia
Exclusive United States Distribution: Sundance Publishing

ISBN 0-7608-9337-3

# Contents

# CENTRAL AMERICA

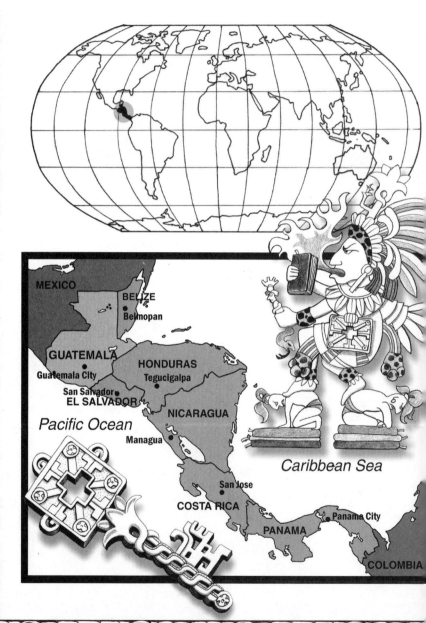

MEXICO

BELIZE
• Belmopan

GUATEMALA
• Guatemala City

San Salvador •
EL SALVADOR

HONDURAS
• Tegucigalpa

NICARAGUA

Pacific Ocean

• Managua

Caribbean Sea

• San Jose
COSTA RICA

• Panama City
PANAMA

COLOMBIA

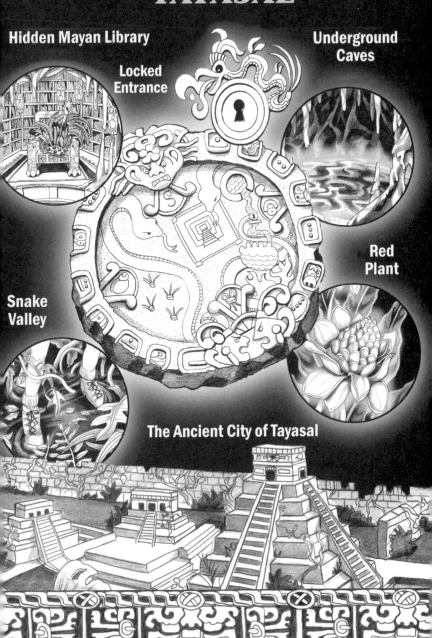

# The LOST LIBRARY of TAYASAL

**Hidden Mayan Library**

**Locked Entrance**

**Underground Caves**

**Red Plant**

**Snake Valley**

**The Ancient City of Tayasal**

# CHAPTER 1

# Kidnapped!

"Your uncle didn't just disappear! I'm sure of it, Mia. He's been kidnapped!" said Ricky.

"Maybe Uncle Earl found something amazing and had to leave in a hurry," suggested Mia.

"Sshhh." Ricky put his hand over Mia's mouth. "We don't want anyone to know what your uncle might have found."

Ricky paced the worn floorboards of the police station. He couldn't keep still . . . he had to do something. The police waiting room was still full of people. Ricky and Mia had already been waiting there for two hours.

"Señor Ricky and Señorita Mia?" a voice called.

"Over here," shouted Ricky. Mia and Ricky pushed their way through the crowd toward the policeman. He was middle-aged, with dark hair, dark eyes, and weathered skin.

"Buenos dias, Señor Ricky and Señorita Mia! My name is Ramirez. Follow me, please."

Mia and Ricky followed Ramirez to a small room.

"Mia, your Uncle Earl has disappeared?"

"Yes, that's right," said Mia. "Last night I was awakened by the wind blowing through my tent. As I stepped outside, I heard muffled screams coming from Uncle Earl's tent. I got Ricky, and we searched for Uncle Earl—but he was gone! Then we came to see you."

Ramirez made quick notes on his notepad. "Now, exactly what was your uncle digging for in the jungle?"

"He thought he had found the remains of a Mayan village." Mia paused for a moment. "But the only things he's dug up so far are some old pieces of broken pottery."

Ramirez looked at both of them, and then his eyes rested on Mia. "So he made no mention of a stone tablet that glowed in the dark?"

"A what? Who's ever heard of glowing stone tablets?" Mia gave a small, nervous laugh.

"I think *you* have, Mia. I'm talking about a stone tablet with a map etched on the front that shows the location of a lost Mayan city—a city that has never been found. Rumor has it that this city contains the lost Mayan Library." Ramirez's voice was beginning to rise.

"Look, sir," Ricky said, cutting in. "I don't know what you are suggesting. Uncle Earl has disappeared, and that's the only reason we are here. We're not here because of a wild goose chase after some glow-in-the-dark magic map."

Ignoring Ricky, Ramirez raised his eyebrows at Mia. He leaned back in his chair before speaking slowly. "I'm sorry about your Uncle Earl, but . . . well, sometimes people disappear around here." He raised his hands and shrugged. "This place can be very dangerous. Perhaps your uncle was looking for something that got him into trouble. At any rate, I cannot help you."

Mia was shocked and blurted out, "What do you mean you can't help? You *have* to help!"

Ramirez's smile was sinister. "Tell me the truth about what your uncle was doing—then I may be of some help to you." He stood and held the door open for them.

Stunned, they walked out into the cool, early morning air. "I don't get it, Mia. Why wouldn't he help?" Ricky asked.

Mia glanced around to make sure no one could hear her. "Because they all want what Uncle Earl may have found—the lost library of the Maya. Some people believe the library holds the answer to how the Mayans built their pyramids. Amazingly, a knife can't penetrate the joints of a Mayan building—so how did they make them that exact?" Mia went on without waiting for an answer. "The Mayans never got sick and lived until they were very old. That may be the really big secret that everyone is looking for. Maybe the library holds the key to eternal life! How would that be for a find?"

"But Uncle Earl doesn't have the tablet, Mia!
He never talked about some old library. He just
wanted to find some pots and stuff!"

"That's where you're wrong, Ricky. Follow me.
I'll show you what Uncle Earl has found."

# CHAPTER 2

# In Search of
# the Lost Library

Mia and Ricky arrived back at the dig site soon after dawn. The moss-covered ruins didn't seem as interesting without Uncle Earl. Ricky scanned the site and looked in each of the tents.

"There's no one left," said Ricky. The site was deserted. They were alone in this enormous jungle.

"The police have been here," said Mia. She handed Ricky an envelope addressed to them. He opened it and read aloud a note.

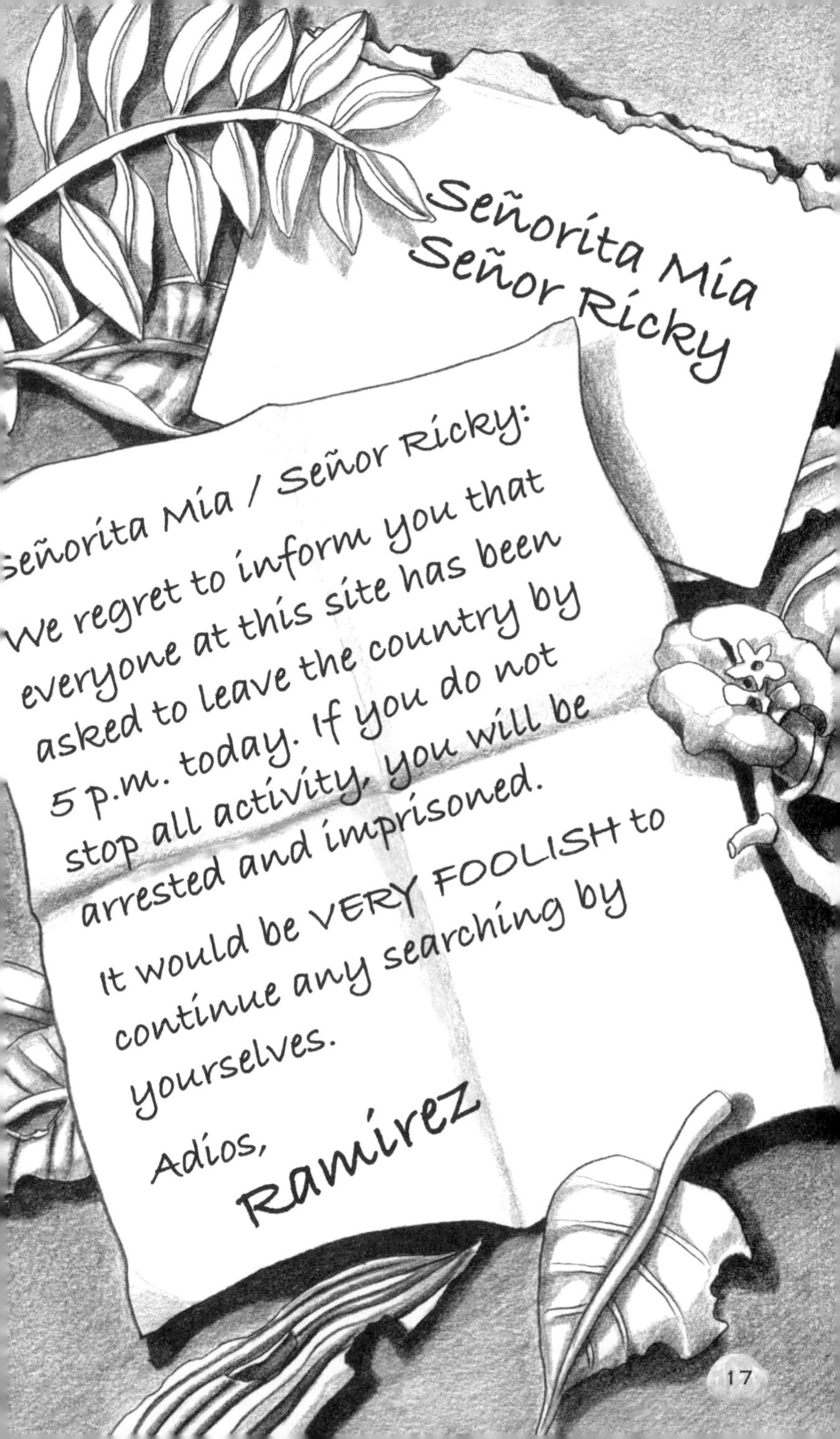

Señorita Mía
Señor Ricky

Señorita Mía / Señor Ricky:

We regret to inform you that everyone at this site has been asked to leave the country by 5 p.m. today. If you do not stop all activity, you will be arrested and imprisoned.

It would be VERY FOOLISH to continue any searching by yourselves.

Adios,

Ramirez

17

"That's a pretty stern warning. I think that we should start to pack up," Ricky said, walking off toward his tent.

"Pack? But Ricky, we can't leave without Uncle Earl!" cried Mia.

Ricky smiled and took a deep breath. "No, silly—pack for an expedition in search of Uncle Earl. Now, tell me what you know."

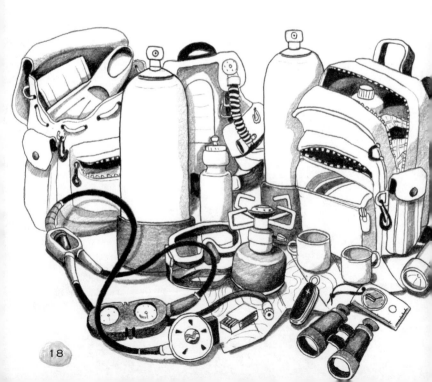

For the next hour, Mia and Ricky packed everything they might need. They knew they should take food, water, hiking and scuba equipment, and other survival gear for their journey. As they packed, Mia told Ricky all she knew.

"So Uncle Earl thinks the lost Mayan Library is hidden in the underground caves?" asked Ricky.

Mia nodded. "It's supposed to be among the largest system of underground caves and rivers in the world. I think Uncle Earl believes the caves would be the perfect hiding place for ancient treasure."

"Why did the Mayans need to hide their treasure?"

"In 1697, the Spanish invaded the city of Tayasal. They were taking everything. The king of the city, King Can Ek, decided to hide all the treasure. He built a magnificent underground city where 2,000 people lived."

"Well, it's a mighty big jungle out there. Do you have any idea where we should start looking?" Ricky asked.

Mia removed a small purple book from her pocket. "I found Uncle Earl's journal. The clues to finding him and the lost library are in here."

Ricky's eyes widened. "Let me have a look!"

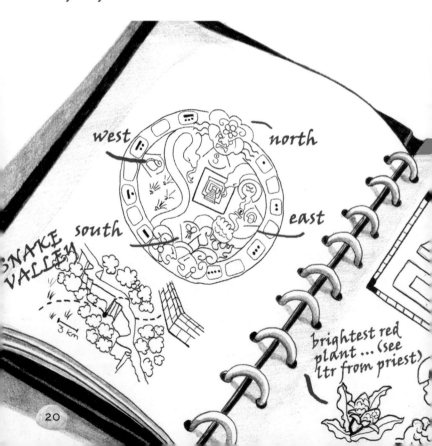

Mia opened to a page of pictures. "See, he's got all the clues recorded. The first clue is the fluorescent stone tablet Ramirez was asking us about. Uncle Earl's been studying it for over a year. It is a map of the ancient library that pinpoints two ancient cities somewhere in Snake Valley. Uncle Earl just discovered the second clue while he was making inquiries at the Hall of Records. He came across a letter written by a priest saying that he had visited the lost library. This priest wrote that it was hidden in caves located behind the brightest red plant in the jungle. The third clue Uncle Earl recorded was this Mayan hieroglyph." Mia turned the page and pointed to a diagram.

ost city
yasal

GUATEMALA CITY
HALL

HALL OF RECORDS
CITY OF GUATEMALA

I had the privilege today, this day 20 August 1745, to be admitted to the secret library of Tayasal. It is well hidden in an underground cave system behind the brightest red plant in the jungle. Although I inquired about this library

ocation of
library
vithin the
ve systems

21

"What does it say, Mia?" asked Ricky.

Suddenly a voice interrupted them. "It's a hieroglyph that means danger, Ricky. The Mayan gods do not want the lost library found."

Mia and Ricky whirled around to see Professor Drake, Uncle Earl's dig partner. He looked as though he was prepared for a hike.

"We thought everyone was gone," Mia said.

Professor Drake smiled. "We can't leave without Earl, can we? He's the reason we're here in the first place."

"So you'll help us search for Uncle Earl?" asked Mia, with relief in her voice.

"I've already started. I know about everything in that journal you're holding. We'd better get going. The quicker we get out of here, the better," said Professor Drake.

Mia looked again at Uncle Earl's journal. The Mayan hieroglyph was terrifying. An angry, fire-breathing god gripped and crushed books and people. A cold shiver ran down Mia's spine. She hoped nothing terrible had happened to her uncle.

# CHAPTER 3

# Into the Jungle

The three of them slashed a trail through the dense jungle, heading for Snake Valley. The sun was climbing higher, and Ricky felt as if he was being grilled. Sweat poured from Mia's brow as she lifted the heavy machete to clear the jungle ahead. She stopped and pulled one of her high-tech gadgets from her backpack.

"What is it this time, Mia?" Ricky teased.

"It's a GPS—a satellite navigation device that pinpoints where we are."

Ricky looked suitably impressed. "So are we on course?"

Mia waited for the GPS to come up with their coordinates. "It shouldn't be much more than five miles to the limestone cliffs. Then we'll have to climb."

"What!" shrieked Ricky. "You mean we have to climb cliffs after struggling through here?" He turned to Professor Drake.

"Don't look at me, Ricky. Mia told me that you love rock climbing! Besides, there is no other way into Snake Valley."

As they struggled on, the jungle became more treacherous. At times they could barely get a foothold in the soft mud of the rain forest floor. Mia stopped to catch her breath. "This humidity is too much. I'm melting. The jungle is so thick, I don't think we'll ever get there!"

Ricky glanced around. It was already well into the afternoon. At this rate, they'd be lucky to make the cliffs by sunset!

Mia stopped for some water and took a chocolate bar from her backpack. She broke off pieces of chocolate for Ricky and Professor Drake.

"You know," said Professor Drake, "the Mayans loved chocolate. It was one of their favorite foods. They pretty much invented it."

"They would've needed it," Ricky sighed, as he rested against a tree. "This jungle sure takes it out of you."

After two more agonizing hours, they finally reached the base of the cliffs. The limestone walls towered above them. Professor Drake slapped Ricky on the back. "Come on, Ricky, this is an easy one. Just watch your footing and hold on tight."

Professor Drake went first, followed by Ricky. Mia came behind, giving instructions, "Look for solid holds, Ricky. Don't look down, and focus!"

Ricky was determined that he was going to conquer this cliff. His spirits soared with each new hold he made. His hands and feet searched for cracks in the rock's surface. He pulled himself higher, foot by foot, until he finally reached the top. Mia was right behind him.

Exhausted, Ricky and Mia sat down. They looked out over the endless jungle that was now edged by a crimson sunset. Professor Drake was already pulling more rope from his backpack and attaching metal clips to his harness.

"What's going on?" quizzed Ricky. "There's nothing more to climb!"

The professor smiled. "You're right, Ricky, but remember the old saying—what goes up, must come down!"

Ricky's relief at reaching the top disappeared. His groans were interrupted by loud bangs coming from the jungle.

"Hit the dirt," called Professor Drake, pushing Ricky to the ground. "Those are gunshots." He pointed to the jungle they had just trekked through. Lights were making their way to the base of the cliff. "Someone is following us. Quickly, we have no time to lose!"

They roped up and began to climb down the other side of the cliff, their hearts racing. At least going down was much faster than climbing up.

# CHAPTER 4

# The Chase Is On

It was dusk as the three of them entered the thick foliage of Snake Valley.

"We'll have to keep going," panted Professor Drake. "They'll find our trail pretty quickly."

"Who could they be, Professor?" asked Mia nervously. "I don't think you've told us everything!"

"You're right, Mia. You both deserve to know the truth. Earl thinks he's found the location of the lost library of the Maya." Professor Drake paused. "But this man called Ramirez would do anything to stop him. So Earl staged his own kidnapping. It was the only way for Earl to get away from Ramirez. It's given him a day's head start."

"Ramirez! That was the policeman we talked to!" Mia exclaimed.

"A policeman *and* a treasure smuggler. Ramirez is a very powerful man. He knows what a rich and incredible find the Mayan Library would be, and he wants it all for himself," Professor Drake explained.

33

"Why didn't Uncle Earl tell us?" asked Mia.

"Too dangerous, Mia. The fewer people who know, the better. Hopefully Earl will find it. Come on. We'd better keep moving."

They struggled on through the fading light. The thick vines made for slow going. Professor Drake was at the front, slashing at any vines in his path. He raised his machete and slashed through a fresh tangle of vines. "Clang!" He hit something other than vines.

"It's a wall of solid rock!" cried Mia. "And it's so long, I can't see where it ends."

The wall was about fifteen feet high and built of massive boulders, some the size of cars. They climbed to the top and could barely believe what lay on the other side—a Mayan city! Although it was almost dark, they could see courtyards and houses. At the center stood a pyramid with a temple at its summit.

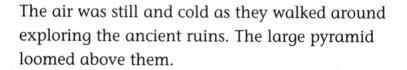

# CHAPTER 5

# The Lost City in the Jungle

The air was still and cold as they walked around exploring the ancient ruins. The large pyramid loomed above them.

"I think we should set up camp and get some sleep. Today has been a long day, and we are sure to have another long one tomorrow," said Professor Drake.

Mia and Ricky didn't argue—they were totally exhausted. They hadn't seen or heard from their pursuers. Hopefully, they were stopping their chase until the next day.

Mia fell asleep right away and began to dream. She dreamed that she was alone in the ancient Mayan ruins. The pyramid was lit a vivid bright green, and she was slowly walking up the stone steps. Black falcons flew in circles high above her. When she reached the top of the pyramid, she made her way into the stone temple. She saw Uncle Earl crouched in a corner of the temple. He turned to Mia and mouthed, "Key."

Mia woke in a cold sweat. She sat upright and called for Ricky.

"Ricky," she whispered. "Wake up, Ricky. We have to go up to the temple!"

Ricky rolled over sleepily and grumbled, "Mia, it's practically the middle of the night!"

"I know that, Ricky, but I think Uncle Earl needs our help right now!"

Ricky jumped up and grabbed their flashlights. They walked through the ancient city to the large central pyramid. On the front face of the pyramid were steep, carved steps that led up to the small stone temple. They ducked their heads to go through the only entrance—a carved, stone doorway leading into the temple.

"Hey! It's slippery, Mia," said Ricky, losing his footing. The temple at the top was exactly as Mia had dreamed. In the darkness, they could just make out brightly colored paintings that covered the walls.

"Look at those, Ricky," said Mia pointing. "Mayan warriors dressed in jaguar skins!"

Ricky scanned the paintings on the walls. "Cool!" he murmured.

Mia walked across to look more closely at one painting. "The Mayans would remove a person's heart as a sacrifice to the gods. This would have been a sacrificial temple."

Goosebumps covered Ricky's arms. "That's awful. Those guys were ferocious."

"Yeah, it was pretty severe," said Mia.

In one corner, Mia found what she was looking for—a glyph carved in the stone wall. "This is it, Ricky. Look! That's the glyph in Uncle Earl's journal. In my dream, Uncle Earl was here, next to this glyph. He said the word *key*. In Mayan temples, there is usually a passageway that leads to the pyramid below. Help me find it!"

Ricky said thoughtfully, "I remember you saying that some hieroglyphs were used to signal the existence of secret passageways. Maybe if we push on this glyph, something will happen! Come on, Mia. Let's try it!"

They both pushed hard and felt the glyph move slightly. There was the sound of stone grinding against stone behind them. Mia and Ricky turned to see that a trapdoor had opened in the middle of the floor. A narrow stairway led down into the heart of the Mayan pyramid.

"Ricky! Look at that!" exclaimed Mia. "Let's go exploring!"

They made their way down the steep stone steps. The light from their flashlights was faint, and once or twice they lost their footing.

At the bottom of the stairs, the floor was covered with green, slimy moss, and water dripped down the walls. In the darkness, one thing caught Mia and Ricky's attention. It was a large golden key laying on a stone slab in the middle of the room.

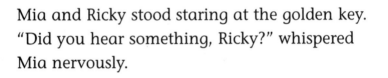

# CHAPTER 6

## The Key and the Plant

Mia and Ricky stood staring at the golden key. "Did you hear something, Ricky?" whispered Mia nervously.

"You've been in the jungle too long, Mia. You're hearing things."

Again, Mia heard a faint noise. It sounded like footsteps on stone. And from the look on Ricky's face, Mia knew that he could hear it now, too.

"Someone's coming down here!" Mia grabbed the key and pulled Ricky into a corner of the chamber.

The footsteps became louder. Then a figure emerged out of the darkness.

"Mia? Ricky? Are you down here?" It was Professor Drake.

"You scared the life out of us!" cried Mia, coming out of the darkness.

"Quickly, both of you! We have to hurry. The hunters are back on our trail. I've been hearing noises in the jungle. We must keep going."

They scrambled back up the steep stairs and raced down the large steps into the cold, night air. At the base of the pyramid, they started to run.

They could all hear voices now.

"Run to the wall. I've got our packs there already," panted Professor Drake. "Then climb!" he yelled.

The crevices in the rock wall were slippery. Ricky's fingers grasped desperately for a good hold. They had reached the top of the wall when a hail of tiny arrows flew after them. One of the arrows hit Mia's backpack; another narrowly missed Ricky's ear. Professor Drake grabbed Ricky's hand and hauled him over. Ricky landed with a hard thud next to Mia.

Ricky pulled the arrow out of Mia's pack.

"Nice shot!" Ricky exclaimed.

"No time to sit around," said Professor Drake, motioning them toward the jungle.

They trekked for about an hour before stopping for a break. Mia showed Professor Drake the golden key.

"It must be the key to the library—the key Uncle Earl wrote about. Here, take a look in his journal, Ricky."

Ricky opened Uncle Earl's purple notebook. Uncle Earl had made a drawing of the key and scrawled an entry:

"To enter the library, a key is needed. The key is thought to be hidden in the ancient city of Tayasal. Tayasal was ruled by King Can Ek, the last of the great Mayan Kings. He moved all the treasure from the city of Tayasal to the hidden caves in Snake Valley. This treasure included the largest library of the ancient Mayans. Legend says that only one with a love of knowledge will be shown where to find the key in the lost city."

King Can Ek

To enter the Library, a key is needed. The key is thought hidden in the ancient city Tayasal. Tayasal was rule King Can Ek, the last of the great Mayan Kings. He move all the treasure from the city of Tayasal to the hidden caves in Snake Valley. This treasure included the largest library of the ancient Mayans. legend says that only one with a l of knowledge will be shown where to find `` key in t

49

"So the glyph was of King Can Ek," Mia said.

Ricky smiled across at her. "You are the chosen one, Mia! You found the key in Tayasal."

Mia smiled, then shrugged. "What good is a key without a door?"

"I think our search is over," exclaimed Professor Drake. "Look over there!" The pair followed the direction of his finger and saw a red glow in the jungle.

"A fire?" asked Ricky.

"No Ricky, a plant! It's the bright red plant," said the professor.

"It's the only plant that glows red. Remember the clue? Behind the plant lies the entrance to the caves. This is the spot!"

"Professor," cried Mia, as she pointed to a ledge, "that looks like a cave up there."

"You're right, Mia. Let's go."

They scrambled up to the ledge and entered the cave. It was gloomy, and the sound of their feet on the rocky ground echoed around them. The cavern was enormous. Parts of it were dimly lit by moonlight filtering through holes in the roof. They searched the cave walls for openings and found five. The three wandered around the cave, not knowing which direction to take.

Ricky could hear a faint sound of rushing water. They picked the opening closest to the sound and followed the passageway as it sloped downward. When they emerged, they found themselves at the top of a thundering waterfall. Carefully, they climbed down beside the rushing water and followed the river around a bend. There it broadened into a calm lake.

"Thank goodness you're here. I've been waiting for you," a voice said.

The three of them stood staring, mouths wide open. Uncle Earl was sitting at the edge of the lake—with a fishing rod!

# CHAPTER 7

# The Glowing Water

"Uncle Earl!" cried Ricky and Mia, running to hug him.

"I thought you'd have found the library by now, Earl," Professor Drake said to his friend. "What stopped you from going on?"

"You forget, Professor, I can't possibly find the library without . . ."

"Without this!" shouted Mia, as she held up the golden key.

"Good girl, Mia. I hoped it would be either you or Ricky who found it. So it's now time to begin the final leg of our search. Do you all have scuba gear?" asked Uncle Earl.

"We've got everything we need," replied Professor Drake.

"Well, I'm guessing that the library is hidden somewhere in this underground cave system," Uncle Earl said.

"But, Uncle Earl," Mia said excitedly, "these underground caves and rivers are like twisted mazes! How will we know where to go?"

"Remember the stone tablet?" asked Uncle Earl.

Mia nodded.

"Well, the tablet produced a strange glow, and the map on the tablet led us here, didn't it?"

Mia nodded again.

"Well, why do you think it glowed?" asked Uncle Earl.

Mia thought hard. For once, she was stumped.

"Maybe because of what it was made of," replied Ricky tentatively.

"Almost right, Ricky," said Uncle Earl. "It glowed because it had been kept in an environment that made it glow."

Mia looked puzzled. "So we're looking for a fluorescent green environment?"

Uncle Earl didn't reply. Instead, he led them along a winding path into another cave with a deep pool—a pool that shimmered fluorescent green. Mia, Ricky, and Professor Drake smiled broadly at each other. They now understood.

Ricky shook his head. "But the library can't really be down there, can it? I mean, how would the Mayans have taken everything through the water?"

"Legend has it," answered Professor Drake, "that they used airtight boxes. Perhaps when we find the library, it will tell us."

It took them a while to gear up. All four had to wear air tanks and underwater headlamps and carry hand-held flashlights. Mia was busy pushing buttons on a new wrist dive computer. Ricky opened his mouth to speak, but decided against it and rolled his eyes instead.

"Professor Drake will go first and mark the way with red underwater markers. You can't surface, so if you get into trouble, follow the markers out. Mia, you hold onto the key," said Uncle Earl.

They plunged into the water one by one. It was calming, like a large, warm bath. Ricky waved his flashlight in front of him. An underwater world of stalactites and stalagmites surrounded them. There were tunnels branching off in different directions. Up ahead, Ricky could see Uncle Earl gesturing madly. He was shining his flashlight onto a far wall. As Ricky swam over, his flashlight swooped across the Mayan glyph they had come to know so well—the glyph of King Can Ek. Below the glyph was a keyhole.

# CHAPTER 8

## Enter the Lost Library

Uncle Earl waved Mia forward so that she could try the key. Mia placed the golden key into the lock. It fit perfectly! Mia turned the key. The heavy stone moved slightly. Uncle Earl and Professor Drake pushed the stone, and it slid back making an opening just large enough for them to swim through.

Ricky gripped his flashlight tightly. The tunnel they were in was completely black. The current started to drag them along quickly. Suddenly they were thrown into a pool of still water. Mia motioned for Ricky to follow her upward.

They broke the surface and removed their masks. They were in a cave lit by hanging gold lanterns. On each wall were shelves of books that reached the ceiling. In the middle of the cave stood a huge throne that was covered by a magnificent feathered headdress.

"It's the library!" yelled Ricky.

Uncle Earl climbed out of the water and walked over to one of the shelves. He carefully lifted up an old parchment.

"What a find," gasped Uncle Earl.

"What a find is exactly right, Earl," hissed a deep voice.

Uncle Earl spun around.

Out of the water jumped Ramirez, smiling broadly. "A magnificent find, Earl. Thank you for leading us to this wonderful library. I have been dreaming of this for a very long time."

Uncle Earl grimaced. "What are you doing here, Ramirez? You think you can sell the contents of this library the way you sell other Mayan artifacts? You're just a thief!"

"In this case, I may get something worth more than money." Ramirez's eyes gleamed. "I may get eternal life."

"Eternal life! What's he talking about, Uncle Earl?" demanded Mia.

Uncle Earl sighed. "Ramirez is talking about an old Mayan myth, Mia. It says that the secret to eternal life is recorded here."

"It's no myth!" shouted Ramirez. "The book must be here. I know it is, and you are going to help me find it." With that command, Ramirez pulled a long dagger from his wetsuit. "Start searching, Earl," he ordered.

"No!" came a thundering voice.

Mia and Ricky froze in panic. Then Mia tugged at Ricky's arm and pointed frantically toward the throne. With a loud swoosh, the headdress of feathers turned to face them. It was no longer just a headdress. There was now a man wearing it! He was dressed in a brightly colored sarong with golden anklets on each foot. His chest was bare, except for a golden Mayan glyph that hung from his neck.

The figure spoke. "No one will take the contents of this library. No book shall leave this cave," his voice boomed.

"Pretty scary librarian," Ricky whispered to Mia. "I wouldn't want to have any overdue books."

Ramirez slowly walked forward with a bowed head. "King Can Ek, we do not wish to take the books, but to learn from them."

"So you know who I am?" bellowed the figure.

"Yes," replied Ramirez. "You are the spirit of King Can Ek, last king of the Maya, guardian of the lost library, possessor of the knowledge of eternal life."

King Can Ek said grimly, "You are a greedy and wicked man, Ramirez! The library cannot be seen by the people of today. You are not ready for our knowledge. There are too many people in your world who would use the knowledge in these books selfishly. People like you." The king fixed his eyes on Ramirez. "This is the end of your journey."

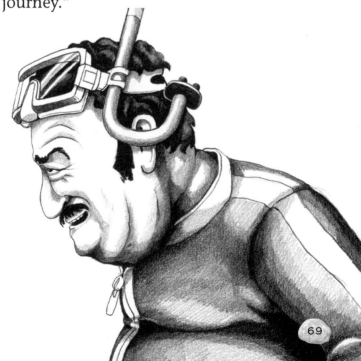

Ramirez was locked in eye contact with the king. Sweat poured from Ramirez's brow, and his whole body started to shake. He looked as though he was burning up from the inside. Suddenly huge jets of fire shot up all around him, licking the ceiling. Then, with a loud roar, the fire stopped as instantly as it had begun. Ramirez had disappeared. The room was silent.

"Ramirez was a bad man," King Can Ek said. "He could never be trusted with the knowledge from this library." The king sighed. "A hundred years ago, I would have ripped his heart out. But I just don't have the energy these days."

"Thank goodness!" croaked Mia.

King Can Ek motioned for Uncle Earl to come forward. "Now, Earl, you are a good and wise man. You have treated our ancient Mayan cities with care. I would like to give you a gift from the library. However, you must promise never to return."

Uncle Earl did not hesitate. "As you wish, King," he stammered, still a little shaken.

King Can Ek rose from his throne, gathered a scroll from the shelf, and gave it to Uncle Earl.

"It is yours to decipher. Take it with you, but tell no one how, or from where, you found it. I can't tell you what it means. I can only say that I think your people have been searching for it for a long time. They will be pleased that you found it." He gave a hearty laugh that filled the library.

# CHAPTER 9

# The Message on the Scroll

*Six Months Later . . .*

Uncle Earl and Professor Drake looked down from the top level of the shopping center to the frenzied crowd below. People were lining up in queues in every direction. Behind the counter, Ricky and Mia were busily serving customers.

"I just can't believe how successful that recipe has been. Since Mia cracked the code on the scroll, people just can't get enough of the stuff," said Professor Drake. "Those Mayans really knew a thing or two about chocolate."

"Oh, I think the name and slogan that Ricky came up with helped," laughed Uncle Earl. He took a bite of a heart-shaped chocolate bar and read aloud from the front of the wrapper, "**Mayan Crunch** The Royal Chocolate Without the Sacrifice."

He nudged the Professor and said, "I think King Can Ek would be very pleased with that."

# THE MAYAN LIBRARY

Deep within the jungles of South America lie the ancient temples and palaces of the Mayan civilization. The Mayans were a race of people who built magnificent cities, were masters at mathematics and astrology, and developed an elaborate writing system.

The Mayan cities survived until 1697, when the last city, Tayasal, was overtaken by Spanish invaders. The king of Tayasal, King Can Ek, and his people vanished into the forest and were never found. They took with them the treasures of the city, including a huge library of Mayan scrolls. These scrolls apparently recorded ancient Mayan medicines, astrology, and the secrets of eternal life. It was believed that King Can Ek took his people and library to caves deep within the Mayan mountains. This cave system is one of the most extensive in the world, consisting of vast underground chambers and underwater passages that modern people have only begun to explore.

In 1994, an American archaeologist stumbled upon a clue to the whereabouts of King Can Ek's library—an ancient glowing stone. This stone tablet revealed an ancient Mayan map and indicated a site in Snake Valley, in Belize. An American archaeological team is presently preparing for an expedition to recover the lost library of the Maya.

Finding the library of the Maya would unravel the mystery surrounding Central America's oldest civilization and may provide answers to some of our most puzzling questions.

# Glossary

**adios** (Spanish) good-bye

**buenos días** (Spanish) good morning

**coordinates** numbers which define the position of something

**crevices** cracks

**focus** concentrate on

**fluorescent** radiation given off as light

**glyph** a hieroglyph, or a carved figure as part of a pictograph

**grimaced** made an ugly facial expression

**harness** straps forming a safety brace

**hieroglyph** a symbol used in a writing system where pictures are used for words

**limestone** a type of rock

**machete** a large, heavy knife

**Mayan** relating to the original people and their descendants who inhabit the Yucatan Peninsula, Guatemala, and Belize

**parchment**  very thick paper; used to be made from animal skins

**penetrate**  pierce through

**queues**  lines of people waiting for something

**sacrificial temple**  where sacrifices of people or animals were made

**scroll**  a roll of parchment

**Señor**  (Spanish) mister; sir; title for a man

**Señorita**  (Spanish) miss; title for an unmarried girl or woman

**stone tablet**  a flat slab or surface made of stone

**vivid**  strikingly bright

# Titles in This Series